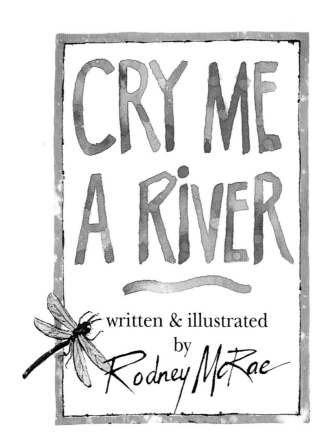

CRY ME A RIVER

written & illustrated
by
Rodney McRae

For my mother, Elaine

An Angus & Robertson Publication

Angus&Robertson, an imprint of
HarperCollins*Publishers*
25 Ryde Road, Pymble, Sydney, NSW 2073, Australia
31 View Road, Glenfield, Auckland 10, New Zealand

First published in Australia in 1991
This Bluegum paperback edition published 1994

National Library of Australia
Cataloguing-in-Publication data:

McRae, Rodney, 1958–

Cry me a river.
ISBN 0 207 17197 1 (hb)
ISBN 0 207 17203 X (pb)

1. Environmental protection—Juvenile literature.
I. Title.

363.7

Printed in Hong Kong

9 8 7 6 5 4 3 2 1
98 97 96 95 94

CRY ME A RIVER

story and Illustrations by Rodney McRae

Angus&Robertson
An imprint of HarperCollins*Publishers*

W

The Mountain stood
at the top of the world
and looked down upon me.

'Cry me a river!' I said
and I watched as shimmering tears
ran down her chiselled features
and around the brittle tussocks
that framed her face
like golden locks of amber hair.

'Cry me a river!' I said
and her tears welled up in crystal pools
and cascaded out over polished stones,
giving life to everything they touched.

'Cry me a river!' I said
and her river of tears met the tree line,
and were soothed by cool green moss
and moist bark and lichen.

'Cry me a river!' I said
and her tears flowed on
through valley and thicket,
growing stronger and richer,
wider and deeper.

'Cry me a river!' I said
and beneath the sparkling surface
of her tears life abounded
and its forms took many shapes and colours.

'Cry me a river!' I said
and her tears became
a soothing playground
for the children of the land
and a quenching fountain
for the animals
of the forest and the fields
and all the birds of the air.

'Cry me a river!' I said
and her tears flowed out upon the clear land
where the trees had once stood.
Her tears grew cloudy as they mixed with
the silt of the land and wasted fertilizer.

'Cry me a river!' I said
and her tears darkened
and weeds flourished in her pain
and choked her with their numbers.

'Cry me a river!' I said
and onward her river of tears
struggled towards the sea,
as the fruits of human progress
discharged themselves into her belly.

'Cry me a river!' I said
but her crystal tears
became like soup,
and no life could be
nourished within them
and her breath became
strong and putrid.

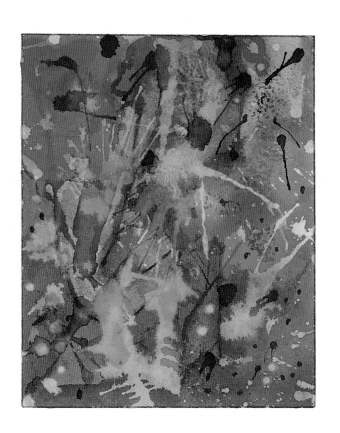

'Cry me a river!' I said
and at last her tears
made union with the sea,
and the wake from her mouth
discoloured her sister,
and forced her to drink poison.

'Cry me a river!' I said
and the Mountain replied.

'My tears are freely given
to an earth that thirsts.

'The sun melts my snowy veil
to bring life to the world,
yet with each new fall of snow
I see less clearly
and my eyes burn with sorrow.
My tears of life are wasted
on the greedy and the careless,
and the sun's rays of hope
are shaded by indifference.'

'So cry *me* a river!' said the Mountain.

So I cried me a river
and I cared for my river
and I ran with my river to the sea.

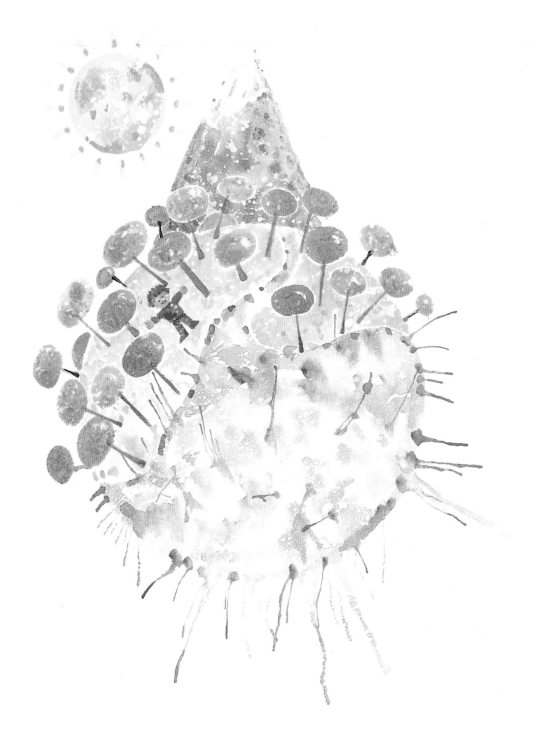

When I reached the sea it became clear.
And I saw that with each new day
a beginning is made
and from each new tear a river is born
and for each new problem a solution is sought.
It's up to you and me!